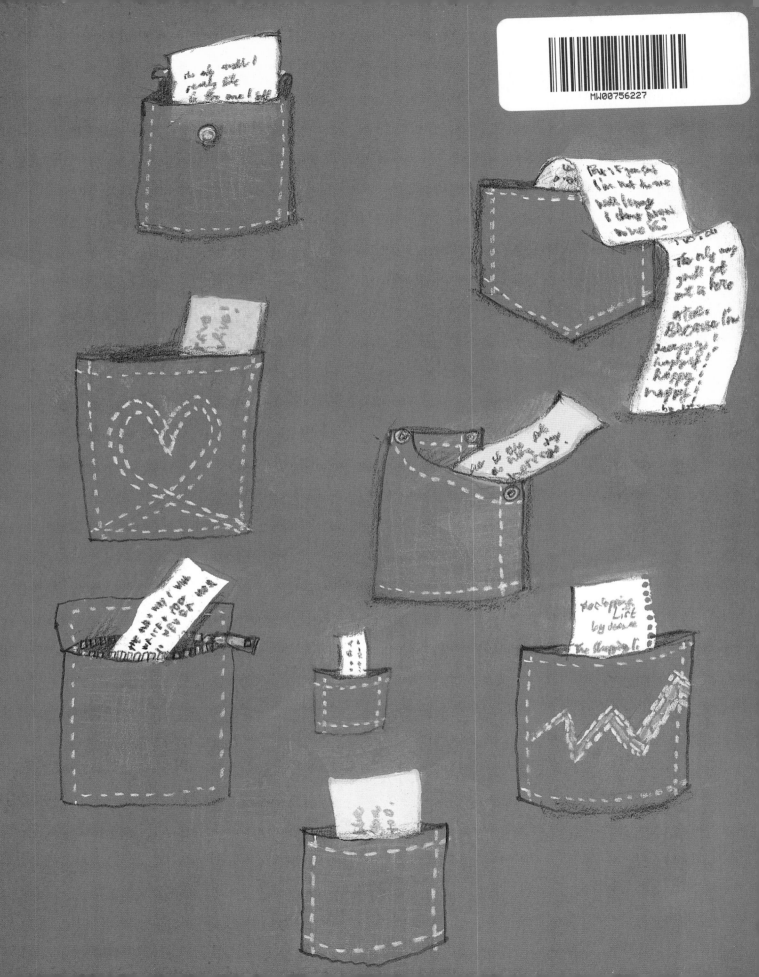

In honor of Miss Joy Glanville —M.M.
For Margaret M. and Brenda B., with love —G.B.K.

The author and artist wish to express their gratitude to the students and
faculty of Greenwich Academy in Greenwich, Connecticut, for inspiring
many of the Poem in Your Pocket Day activities in this book.

Text copyright © 2015 by Margaret McNamara
Jacket art and interior illustrations copyright © 2015 by G. Brian Karas
All rights reserved. Published in the United States by Schwartz & Wade Books, an imprint of
Random House Children's Books, a division of Random House LLC, a Penguin Random House Company, New York.
Schwartz & Wade Books and the colophon are trademarks of Random House LLC.
Visit us on the Web! randomhousekids.com
Educators and librarians, for a variety of teaching tools, visit us at RHTeachersLibrarians.com

Library of Congress Cataloging-in-Publication Data
McNamara, Margaret.
A poem in your pocket / by Margaret McNamara ; illustrated by G. Brian Karas. — First edition.
pages cm
Summary: Elinor is used to doing very well in school, but as Poem in Your Pocket Day approaches,
bringing an opportunity to meet a real poet, her struggle to write a perfect poem causes Elinor's confidence
to falter, despite Mr. Tiffin's guidance and reassurance.
ISBN 978-0-307-97947-6 (hc) — ISBN 978-0-307-97948-3 (glb) — ISBN 978-0-307-97949-0 (ebook)
[1. Poetry—Fiction. 2. Schools—Fiction. 3. Authorship—Fiction. 4. Self-confidence—Fiction.]
I. Karas, G. Brian, illustrator. II. Title.
PZ7.M47879343 Poe 2015
[Fic]—dc23
2014005745

The text of this book is set in Century Schoolbook.
The illustrations were rendered in gouache, acrylic and pencil.
Book design by Rachael Cole
MANUFACTURED IN CHINA
2 4 6 8 10 9 7 5 3 1
First Edition

a Poem in Your Pocket

Margaret McNamara and G. Brian Karas

schwartz & wade books • new york

Mr. Tiffin's class had never had an author visit them before.
"Emmy Crane is a poet," said Mr. Tiffin.

"And she doesn't know it!" said Robert. "That rhymes!"
"Not all poems rhyme," said Elinor.

"Ms. Crane is coming to visit for Poem in Your Pocket Day,"
said Mr. Tiffin. "We're going to write poems of our own and put
them in our pockets."

"I'm going to wear my jeans with six pockets that day," Elinor whispered to Molly. "I'm going to have a different poem in each one."

"I'm sure your poems will be perfect," Molly whispered back.

Elinor thought it would be too show-offy to agree, so she didn't say a word. But inside, she nodded.

Elinor got to work. All during March, she studied poetry.

All during April, the class caught up with Elinor.

They read poetry books and learned poems by heart and wrote poems in their poetry journals.

Every day there was something new to learn.

Mr. Tiffin taught them about similes, and they tried them out.

"Robert is as tall as that really high building in the middle of town!" said Robert.

"Math is like a knot," said Tara.

"One that we can untangle together," said Mr. Tiffin.

A SIMILE compares two different things, using "like" or "as."

They worked on metaphors.

A METAPHOR is a Comparison saying one thing is another.

"Recess is an ice cream cone on a hot day," said Alex. "Even in April."
"Homework is a belt that's too tight," said Jake.

"Do you have a metaphor, Elinor?" asked Mr. Tiffin.

"I'm coming up with something amazing," said Elinor. "I'm just not ready to say anything."

"Elinor is a library," said Tara, "filled with silence."

The class read short poems.
"These are called haiku," said Elinor.
"Little poems can say a lot," said Charlie.
They read puzzle poems. "These are called acrostics," said Elinor.
"They're fun to figure out," said Jeremy.

Haiku
by Jeremy

No more gray days with
A poem in my pocket—
Bright secret rainbow.

Acrostic
by Everybody

Teacher:
Interested,
Friendly,
Fun,
Impressive,
Nice.

They read poems that looked like pictures. "These are called concrete poems," said Elinor.

"A concrete pumpkin seed!" said Kimmy.

And they read a whole lot of funny poems. "Hey, who knew poems could make you laugh?" said Jake.

"I don't know the name for these," said Elinor.

"Whew!" said Molly.

Concrete
by Charlie

There is only one way to find out how many seeds are in a pumpkin; count count count count count count count count count count count count.

Funny
Mom's Complaint
by Jake

We're out of apples, kids—again!
Don't eat so many, please.
they're costing me a lot of dough.
You think they grow on trees?

One bright morning, Mr. Tiffin took the class outside.
"What do you see?" he asked. "Use your poet's eyes."

Everyone looked around.

"Buds are like tiny red
firecrackers," said Charlie,
"waiting to explode into flowers."

"Sadness is a cracked
sidewalk," said Tara.
"Very nice!" said
Mr. Tiffin. "Ms. Crane will
be so impressed." He noticed
that Elinor was being very
quiet. "How about you,
Elinor? What does your
poet's eye see?"
Elinor wanted Ms. Crane
to be impressed with her, too.
"I'm still thinking," she said.

One Friday afternoon, Mr. Tiffin brought everyone in class a small brown bag with a surprise inside.

"Sneak a peek inside your bags and then write a poem about what's in there. But don't tell anyone what you're writing about," he said. "We'll do our best to guess."

The class took out their poetry journals and got to work.

Then they read their poems out loud.

Alex guessed that Jake had a pebble in his bag, and she was right.

Kimmy guessed that Molly had a glass animal, and she was right. She could even tell that it was a horse.

No one could guess what Elinor had in her brown bag. Her journal page was clean and blank. "This shell is too perfect to write about," she said.

"Try again at home tonight," said Mr. Tiffin. "And remember, poetry is a messy business."

On Saturday night, Elinor tried to finish her brown-bag poem. She wrote seven drafts, and she only liked one. When she woke up in the morning, she read the poem she'd liked. "This stinks!" she said.

On Sunday night, Elinor wrote six haiku, with a total of three metaphors and two similes. She smiled as she went to bed.

In the morning, she looked them over. "These are not poetry!" she said.

By Monday night, Elinor was worried. She wrote eleven rhyming poems.

The next morning, she threw them off her desk.

"Today is Poem in Your Pocket Day," she said. "And I don't have anything that's good enough!"

Elinor's eyes stung as she got ready for school. She wore a dress with just one small pocket, with nothing inside it. The day was as gray as Elinor's mood.

The whole school was decorated for Poem in Your Pocket Day. There were pockets on the doors and poems in those pockets. There were pockets on the lockers and poems stuffed in those. There were rolled-up poems and stapled poems. There was a poem written in chalk on the sidewalk, but that one had run in the rain.

All the students had
poems in their pockets.
All except one.

Elinor worked on her poem at recess.

She worked on her poem in the girls' room.

She even worked on her poem during science. But the more she worked, the harder it was to think.

At the end of the day, the students gathered in the gym for the poetry assembly. Mr. Tiffin told the school that Emmy Crane was "a great American poet." He led her to the stage and she sat down in the Author's Chair.

"She looks like a queen!" said Molly.
"She looks perfect," said Elinor.

Emmy Crane read some of her poems aloud. She told the students what it was like to be a writer and answered their questions.

"Do you make a lot of money?" asked Robert.

"Just enough," said Emmy Crane.

"Where do you get your ideas?" asked Charlie.

"From everything I think and everything I feel," said Emmy Crane.

At last it was time for Mr. Tiffin's class to read their poems. Elinor could hardly breathe as her classmates went up onto the stage and pulled their poems out of their pockets.

Charlie recited his poem.
Emmy Crane grinned.

Robert shouted his poem.
Emmy Crane winked.

Tara whispered her poem.
Emmy Crane nodded.

Finally, it was Elinor's turn. She looked at Mr. Tiffin. "Would you rather not read your poem?" he asked.

Elinor could not even speak. "I wanted my poem to be perfect," she said to Mr. Tiffin. "But I have nothing in my pocket. Nothing at all."

"You don't have to go up there," said Mr. Tiffin.

"I can't disappoint Emmy Crane," said Elinor.

Elinor walked slowly up onto the stage.

She looked out at all the students and all the teachers and at Emmy Crane herself.

"My name is Elinor," she said in a tiny voice, "and I don't have a poem in my pocket. I tried and tried, but I couldn't get it right."

"Come over here, Elinor." Emmy Crane smiled a small smile as Elinor walked closer. "No poem is perfect," she said, in a voice only Elinor could hear.

"I thought of so many things!" Elinor told Emmy Crane. "But they're all in my head."

"Tell me what you've been thinking about, Elinor," said Emmy Crane.

Elinor closed her eyes and thought about the poems she wanted to write.

"I have a poem," she said,
"in the pocket of my mind." She
remembered the poetry books she
had studied at the library. "It is
neat and perfect there. . . ."

She used her poet's eye. "As delicate
as a shell, and as sturdy."
She thought about the treasure
in her brown bag. "It has mysteries
hidden inside it."

Then she thought about her blank
journal page. "But when I try to
write it down, the words disappear."
She pictured the poem on the
sidewalk that morning. "Like chalk
on the sidewalk in the rain."
Then she opened her eyes.

At last Emmy Crane spoke. "That's a poem itself," she said to Elinor. "Those are words from the heart, and words from the heart are where poetry begins."

Elinor stepped down from the stage. The assembly was over.

Everybody clapped and cheered for Emmy Crane.
Elinor was feeling too much to cheer, so she cheered
inside, as loud as she could.

Elinor's Poetry Page

 Poetry doesn't have to rhyme.

 Poems can come to you anytime.

 Follow your ideas wherever they may wind.

 Keep a poem in the pocket of your mind.

- April is National Poetry Month, but poetry is year-round.

- Poem in Your Pocket Day is generally celebrated in the third week of April. Set a date that works for your school, or join in with local or national festivities.

- Make pockets out of construction paper and hang them in your classroom. Fill the pockets with poetry on the big day.

- Ask older students to read their pocketed poems to younger students as part of the day's celebration.

- Encourage faculty and staff to carry poems in their own pockets. No one is too old or too important for poetry.

- Take time to memorize a poem or two with your class. Poems learned by heart stay with you for a long time.

Mr. Tiffin's Pointers